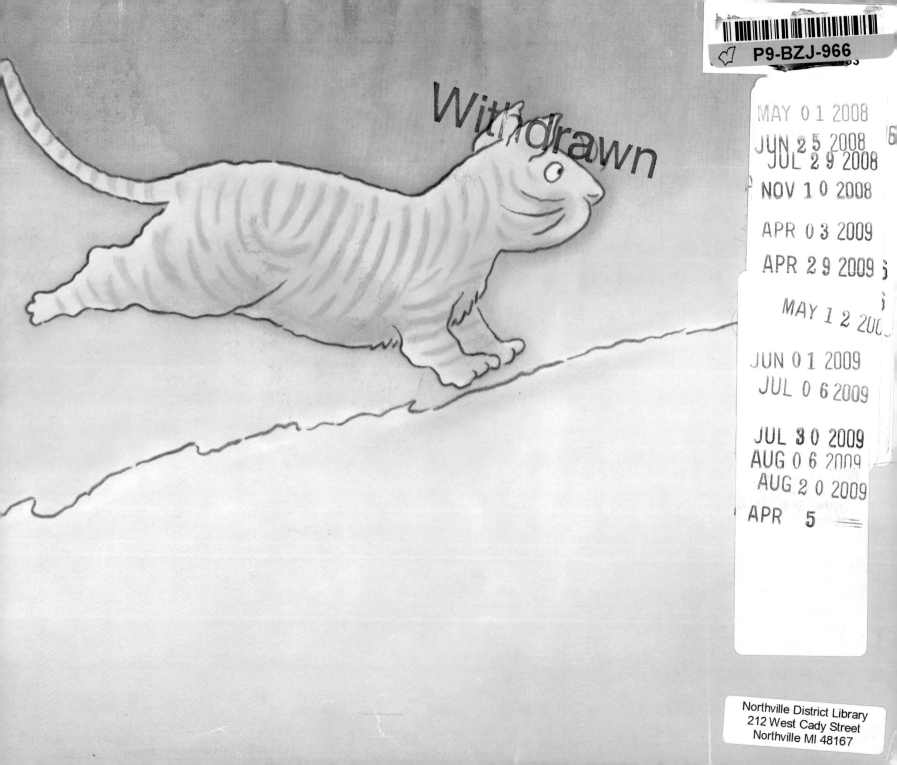

Wake Up, It's Spring!

Wake Up, It's Spring!

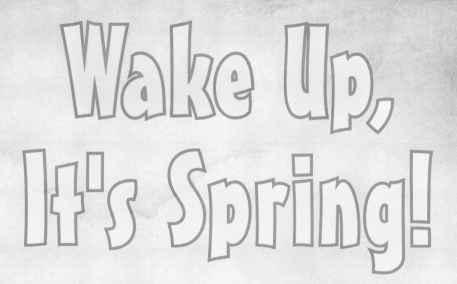

By Lisa Campbell Ernst

HarperCollins*Publishers*

Wake Up, It's Spring!

Copyright © 2004 by Lisa Campbell Ernst

Manufactured in China by South China Printing Company Ltd.

All rights reserved.

www.harperchildrens.com

Library of Congress Cataloging-in-Publication Data

Ernst, Lisa Campbell.

Wake up, it's spring! / by Lisa Campbell Ernst.

p.   cm.

Summary: Word of the arrival of spring spreads
from earth to worm to seed to lady bug and on through
the natural world to a sleeping family, until everyone is
dancing in celebration.

ISBN 0-06-008985-7 — ISBN 0-06-008986-5 (lib. bdg.)

[1. Spring—Fiction.   2. Animals—Fiction.   3. Nature—Fiction.]   I. Title.

PZ7.E7323 Sp   2004   [E]—dc21   2002068733

Typography by Neil Swaab

1 2 3 4 5 6 7 8 9 10

❖

First Edition

To my mom

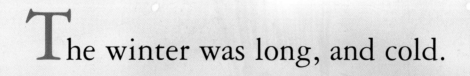

The winter was long, and cold.

Then early one morning
the sun rose and warmed the earth.
"Wake up, old friend, it's Spring!"
whispered the sun.

And the warmed earth woke up.

The earth basked in the sun's glow,
then nudged its guest, the earthworm.
"Time to wake up. Spring is here!"

And the earthworm woke up.

The worm wiggled in the warm
earth and sang to its neighbor, the seed:
"Spring is here! Rise and shine!"

And the seed woke up.

The seed sprouted, and grew out of
the earth. It called to the sleeping ladybug,
"Wake up! Spread your wings. It is Spring!"

And the ladybug woke up.

The ladybug laughed in the sunshine.

It tickled the rabbit's ear as it whispered,

"*Pssst*—rabbit! Spring is here!"

And the rabbit woke up.

The rabbit twitched his nose to smell the Spring
air. He thumped to the bird up in her nest.
"Out of bed, sleepyhead. It's Spring!"

And the bird woke up.

The bird soared from above and flew
past the sleeping cat. "Wake up, furry friend,"
the bird chirped. "Spring is here!"

And the cat
woke up.

The cat s-t-r-e-t-c-h-e-d her legs
and rubbed past the sleeping dog.
"Time to get up."
She yawned.
"It's Spring."

And the dog woke up.

The dog frisked and jumped and barked into the baby's room. "Wake up! Wake up! It's Spring!" cheered the dog.

And the baby woke up.

The baby stood up in her crib with a laugh and shouted to her brother and sister, "Out! Out! Spring!"

And the
brother and
sister woke up.

They picked up the baby and ran to their parents' room, jumped on the bed, and shouted, "Wake up! Open your eyes! Spring is here! Spring is here at last!"

And the parents woke up.

(One eye at a time.)

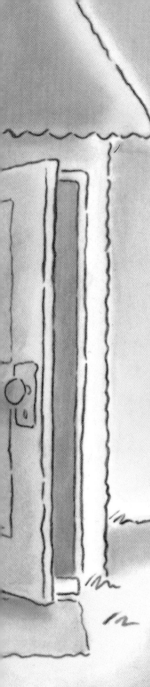

And they all ran to dance together in the sun—

the parents

and the brother and sister

and the baby

and the dog

and the cat

and the bird

and the rabbit

and the ladybug

and the seed

and the worm

and all the earth—

because it was *SPRING*!